AF451606

The Warmth of the Rain

antara

First published by Writer's Pocket in 2024

email: publish@writerspocket.com

ISBN-13: 978-93-6083-417-3

www.writerspocket.com

To everyone who is here or not, but loves me unconditionally.

CONTENTS

This world and its people are transforming as time passes. In the grand ruse of things, nothing really matters. Happiness and success are just temporary waves in the vast ocean of life.

As I steer through this ocean, I am searching for something that I have lost, something that is essential to me. I am just another wave in this sea, and I dedicate this piece to all the lives that surround me.

I'm tying us in an unconditional bond,
With some of my emotions and some of yours
Let's fly together to an unknown sky
With joy, smile, fear, excitement, sorrow & tears!

Little Gratitude

Light is coming to my eyes
My brain starts working, figuring out what's
going on;
Then I open my eyes to the sun
From my east-side window, he has come
To make another day good for me
I look here and there, searching my room,
To leave my bed, I sit looking at myself
I squint, and I go down
My feet touch the floor;
It is cold, and I can feel
It's not a good feeling, I know
Still, I am very grateful
Today, I can stand on my feet,
Feel the senses through my body,
Is it anything less than a blessing?
No, not for me!

Thousands of people are living
Unable to find this joy;
Every minute, they deprive
They are more like a toy!
Their luck is not there, not holding their hand
Little joy over the tiniest thing is so hard,
So hard for them to enjoy
Twenty-four is ninety-six for some,
For others, is one

Every single moment is precious for some,
The world is not pretty for all at all!

Counting me not in them is another reason to live
Living is a blessing for me
Thus, I want to grow and thrive
I am still living here, all fit and fine
In any way, I can do anything,
Without thinking for a second time
I can do whatever I wish to
Every day is good for me!

'Was' All Mine

Ten years! After ten years, I visited this place,
It was the place I once used to call home!
Addresses in many documents will lead here till
today
It is just a house of bricks, tiles, and furniture
Making it only a frame!
The home is gone, with people making it home!
I never wanted to revisit this place to walk the
same path I once left;

A nightmare led me to take the possibly first
train
Telling no one I had come here secretly!

Rusty keys in my hand, perfectly fitted in that
keyhole again
Sunlit my place, looking at me
The same way it used to be
My eyes were not stable,
Searching for something was lost years ago!

I came to my senses when my feet stepped on my
favorite piece, a pen
Was used for the last time ten years back
But the time was to find my room, find my guitar
That called me, pulled me here to free it
Dust was an inch thick, and spiders made it their

home
I got this as a gift on my twelfth birthday,
It was dearest of mine
Cleaning the dust with my hands,
I hugged it close
"Today, I'll take you with me,
You will never be alone!"

Its shine has lessened by a little, and two strings
have torn
It didn't matter
My favorite is my favorite, all-time in all!

I looked around to see some more
Ask about them
How had they been standing there
Without hoping for years and years and more?
But my beating heart was racing,
I couldn't stand it anymore!

Taking the guitar in my hand
I ran to close the door
Speeding up my feet, I ran away without looking
back
My dearest is in my hand
All I needed was to live some years more!

People with bigger hearts
Longer goes, they say
I'm living in the storm
I can't agree to the same!

A New

Is it a crack? Or isn't it?
The part of joining is breaking,
My old skin is shedding
Slowly, with squeaks,
But mine don't sound
One piece with the other
Years of shackles are falling,
Falling apart, one, two, three
Pieces are piling up, uncountable, and
immeasurable

I am looking at, looking at turning my head
My whole body is a new
A new I is forming from me

And
All I can see is a heap, a heap that I can't leap
As if I don't want to,
For the last time, I am trying to hold me back
But it's over, and my body is free now
All of them are ashes now
No more backing up
No more showing less

To be Free

Do I need to prove you again?
Do I need to go?
Do I need to make me feel,
That I felt just a while ago?

Why are you that ruthless?
Is it fun, really?
Do you feel the same joy
In the same game, you've begun?

I am the victim
I can't say that;
I chose you to choose me
I was the one!

Seeing me go to hell
I will hit you with the real,
That's what I thought
But for you, it's not a big deal!

A daily play for you, it can be
It isn't for me
Thriving through hell, again and again,
I want to be free!

It's December, it's getting cold
It's tough for me to walk alone
Without your hands to hold!

Where Souls Meet

The sun is gone, and so is the moon
It's a starry night with you and me
Sitting by the side, not going anywhere
Our fun is in silence, and emptiness is feeling us!

I lose my words when I come close to you
It may not be the same for you,
Now that you've done with all your talks and tales
It's my turn to show me to you

I am holding you, taking your hand in mine,
Feeling it through all my senses,
Not only depending on the eyes
Your skin is so close to me like you're mine
Keeping you inside me, not only in my mind
People live in people's minds, even when they die!

Do you feel strange? Is it scaring you?
Have I mistakenly shown you the side I'm insecure?
Is it the same for me as it was nine years ago
Even today, I feel as anxious as I felt that night and
the next day too!

Now that it comes to the cause, you'd ask?
It's an effect of the fear, the pain, the ache I have
gone through!

"What is it?" your pitch was higher,

For some decibels or so
I can't utter a word, nor do I want to!
I leave your hand and put it on your lap,
Bending my head slapped me in the mind thousands
and thousands of times
For not doing what I should do!

The fear is overwhelming, increasing day by day
You are so precious to me that I can't even say,
I am the one who mixes up the things that should
never
Once a thing is gone, it's gone, and that won't come
back,
Even if I try forever
Neither does it repeat,
I believe in my karma and do in myself!

"And what if you lose him, just like you did them
back then?"
A black thought stings my head, but not anymore
It's time for me, at least to try, to let everything go

Smiling at you, I hold your hand again, not doing
the same
This time we are going back, as it's started to rain!

Aching

On the left side of my shoulder
A fine line of pain
Increasing hourly and going up
Aching my head and covering all my thoughts

The hell in this heaven
That keeps crawling me back
To the place that I left
No, it's not just pain

It will cure with a dose of meds
It comes every time, taking all the hell
I want to leave and move
It's gruesome to have

All I want is to lift myself from this
I want to dive deep into the waves of light
No weight will wait for me, and I will fly!

The smell is everything that is left,
Your smell is in my memory
These days, I try to find them
From this to that story!

Fear to Me

Fear is to lose some,
To lose what you have earned
Fear is not able to do
Not going according to plans

Right?
Sounds good?
No, great, actually

No, I am not mocking
Nor telling fear is 'good'!
It was a sigh that you are still in a reasonable
area
Where you can define it

But what will happen when you step out?
Like all those terms listed in the definition of
fear,
No longer applicable to you!
Will you still be feared?
Yes?
Of what?

Sinking Shimmer

Is it only grief?
Am I the only one sinking?
Is it a happy flow?
Rainbow beams tear my heart
Such a surreal place
Oh! Nice to be

Did you notice the same thing?
That thing on repeat
Yeah, that is where we meet
Me inside you, and you inside me!

Such a happy wave
My hands, my legs, and my limbs are floating
My eyes are closed, they can't see,
They only feel, rings and laces of lights
Of different colors
Don't know it's a dream
The only reality I believe
Where do four colors merge
And make a picture of thee

Huh! It's grief, I believe
It's only grief
With the hands of minutes
I am sinking and floating again.

Some things go
They fly above a little more, and then,
They never come back
They go forever;
And back at home
What is left
Only left-back
Holding some faded memories of faded smiles!

Madman

Is he crazy?
Is he a genius?
Is he doing all for me?

It's been two years
And I still wonder
How does he come to me?

Seeing him laugh
Seeing him dance
Seeing him sing and
Seeing him do all the crazy things
I realize
I'm the happiest person in the world
Just being able to be with him

Is it love?
I'm not sure
Is it admiration?
I guess so!
The word is meaningless
When the feelings are overpowering.

Through the Walk Again

It's hard to write,
Hard to cross all the fiery ways I've gone through
Once again, to make it a walk
Memorable, worthy enough to
Make sense for even fifty or hundred years to go!

But the difference lies in experience, they say,
The difference is the way I am,
All of me is different
That day was in the past,
I am just traveling through it
Going to a screening of a show,
Of it, once I was the hero

Hurting the same wound feels like an
unnecessary dig
But to make a monument,
I had to cut open the steps once I buried!

Now the fire doesn't burn, nor do I get chills
from the snow
I am acting again just like in the past, cause it's
just for the show!
As the clock ticks, all sayings come true
This time is hell, not be the same,
Once I pass it through!

Fly me high above the altitude
From where I can never find
The room I had to leave once
Not knowing the reason

Time: You are Slipping

Where the sun meets the sea,
Two figures stand, bent and gray
Once strong and proud, they fought life's fray,
Now frail and weary, they face each day

Their eyes, once bright, now dimmed by time,
Reflect on memories of joys long left behind
Their hair, once full of vigor and pride,
Now thin and wispy, like the autumn wind

Their hands, once calloused from labor's grasp,
Now soft and wrinkled, worn by age's caress
Their voices, once booming loud and clear,
Now faint and trembling, whispering fears

Yet in their hearts, a fire still burns,
A flame that flickers but never expires.
For though their bodies weakened, spirits soar,
And love for life forever endures

Weekend Blues

Long weekdays are not that long for me
As the weekends are
You can call it weekend blue
But I named it
The dark me!
It is the shade of me that I don't want to show
Either to myself or to the world

Starting on Friday morning,
Even on Thursday night
Keep bothering me,
Poking me in the weakest part
Telling me those dirtiest words that nobody
would hear!

I am running from it as fast as I can
But it is more powerful,
Or have I overestimated mine
Has the immense power to stop my activity
It just ruins, snatches me away!

The pain is so aching
And I am huffing
To find my pace
Not be behind the race!

When the mind is darker than the sky
Cloud is over the top
Rain is needed, with a storm
To make again blue, clear, and fine.

Moonless Night

*On nights without the moon, the stars shine
bright,*
A canopy of twinkling lights was in sight
The world is hushed, slumbering deep,
As if nature's voice in sleep does creep!

The darkness reigns supreme, untamed,
Without the lunar glow to proclaim
Its power and grace, the night's own pace
It is set by whispers, soft and low, in place

The shadows dance upon the ground,
Ethereal silhouettes all around
The leaves are shaking with the breeze,
Speaking with only you and me

The nocturnal creatures stir and play,
Under the cover of the starry ray
Their footsteps are quiet on the soil,
As they roam, their secrets are revealed

On nights without the moon, we find our way,
By the light of the stars that guide us every day
And though the lunar glow may be gone,
Our hearts still sing a song.

Floating

The day started with hundreds and thousands of
bubbles
Bubble of emotions and thoughts
With a new day, new energy generates
Leading to a whole new concept of life
But they all encircle the same pattern
I think it is a problem with my brain

With the blink of an eye, time flows in this way
When a new day turns into a new week
Taking me away from myself, far and far away
Neither did I try to force them nor try to control
I am just floating through them just like a
sailor;
Sailing through a stormy sea.

Are they controlling me?
Or am I the controller?
Repeated words are making my world cloudier,
Oh! It's so gloomy these days
With the sun, my soul is dying together with
dusky green!

In deep shadows, hate finds its home,
A poisonous seed that is often sown.
It clouds the heart, dims the light,
Turning a day into an endless night;
Yet love's embrace can break hate's hold,
In kindness, warmth, and bold power

The Eyes

I am wandering through all the pages
All the images show up and down
Stuck in a mundane finger-tapping
Stopped, passed, and again came back
To get stuck only by your eyes!

They say eyes are the mirror of one
What they say is true,
It is impossible to measure the depth
That I can dive into yours through!

They are beautiful to some
Maybe not to some
Will I care even for a second?
No, never, and neither in my lifetime

When it comes to painting your eyes for you
Take a brush, stroke some lines
Like a wave passing through
Make it curvy, make it sparkle
Fill it with all your love
Even that isn't enough
The eyes that I have seen in you

The prettiest would be less
The brightest can't even come close
Maybe the happiest is an inch closer

The same would 'peacefully' do

They rise a length above
When you smile
They give me the peace that I need
When I see you!

It's not the Same You

It is the start, and I have come this far
Leaving your hand won't be possible ever
You were the savior of life

You are the star
You are here but, still not with me
Living under the same roof
But not the same you;
You used to be

It is sad, and I'm hurt, but that won't change
anything
I'm seeing a great man become
The mere piece of being
That person is gone from us,
That man is missing!

Are you that old?
Are you that sick?
Is your ego growing?
Growing like a mammoth,
Taking your soul overpowering!

Whispers in the wind,
Possession's grip tightens, holds,
Lost souls are never free

Feathers and Fantasies

In a world beyond my wildest dreams,
Where reality bends like a twisted scheme,
I lived through moments so absurd and strange,
Weirder than fiction, a tale to arrange.

One day, I woke up with feathers on my head,
And I found myself floating above my bed,
Colorful birds filled my room,
Singing songs that no one else had heard.

I tried to speak, but my voice was gone,
Replaced by chirps and trills, all wrong,
My body felt as light as a feather too
Floating high, with nothing to do.

I looked around and saw rare creatures,
A dragonfly with wings of purple air,
A cat with fur that shimmered brightly,
And flowers that danced with delight.

In this surreal landscape, I did stray,
With every step, a new surprise waited for me
each day,
From giant mushrooms to talking trees,
Each wonder is more unbelievable than the last
degree.

But then, just as suddenly as it began,
Reality returned, and I landed again,
Back in my bed, with no trace left behind,
Of those magical moments, oh so kind.

Though they say the truth is stranger than
fiction,
This experience defied any imagination,
It was weirder than fiction, pure and true,
A memory etched deep within my heart, forever
anew.

Mostly it is Grey

In numbness, I find myself lost in a sea of
emptiness,
A world without feeling, where joy and sorrow
cease to exist.
Every sensation dulled, my heart beats but once a
minute,
As if time itself has slowed down its pace and has
taken a seat.

My mind is a canvas, devoid of any hue or shade,
A blank slate, untouched by the brushstrokes of
life's nuances.
No laughter echoes through these halls, no tears
are shed,
Just an endless silence hanging heavy on my
head.

I move through days like a ghost, a mere specter
of what once was,
A shadow of a soul that drained of all its grace.
Each step I take feels weightless, I am floating
above the ground,
But beneath me lies the truth - a hollow
profound.

Numbness, oh numbness, how you consume my
every thought,

*Leaving me adrift in this vast ocean of
indifference.
I search for solace, for something to make me
whole again,
But your grasp only tightens, leaving me numb
until the end.*

Life is crucial, and so is the earth
But it's our home from where we can start

Each One of You

My days of youth, I knew a young lady so fair,
With chuckling, shinning, and hair like golden
air.
We danced underneath the stars, our hearts so
light,
But time took her far away from my sight.

I once had a friend, a boy so true,
His eyes were blue and, his heart was anew.
We shared our dreams, our hopes, and our fears,
But time took him without tears.

A colleague once, a man so wise,
With words that lit up starry skies.
We worked together, side by side,
But then he left, and I couldn't hide.

In college lobbies, I met a soul so kind,
Who sang with a voice so immaculate and fine!
We studied late, our minds entwined,
But graduation came, and we declined.

In every face, a story unfolds,
Of lives that intertwine and unfold.
Though time may take them a distance apart,
Each one will always hold a chunk of my heart.

When Pain is Real

When pain is burning, and life is waveless
Staying up all night
I always think about what I shouldn't do
And what I should have
My eyes stay open for me
And a lone heart
Do we all feel the same
All night looking at the stars?

We are fated but not connected
We are together, but still not with each other
Like united shoelaces.

Still

In this eerie, timeless moment, I find myself
alone,
The world around me, motionless, like a stone.
The clock has stopped ticking, time stands still,
And all the people are frozen, their faces are so
thrilled.

The trees hold their branches suspended in
midair,
The wind ceases to blow, and silence is
everywhere.
The sun hangs low, its rays are no longer bright,
It was a surreal scene, both strange and quite
tight.

I look around and see the world in pause,
No movement, noise, or any cause.
The buildings stand, their walls unyielding,
As if they had been petrified long.

The cars remain on the roads, their wheels locked
fast,
Their engines are dead, and their journeys have
passed.
The birds sit silent, their songs are unsung,
Their wings were not moving as if they'd been
stung.

But in this frozen moment, I am free
To roam and explore, wild and carefree.
I wander through the streets without a sound,
Feeling weightless, like a ghostly bond.

I climb high buildings and touch the sky,
And look out over the city, feeling spry.
I dance among the trees, my footsteps light,
My heart is filled with joy and pure delight.

For in this timeless moment, I am king,
Master of this world, where all is still.
And though it may not last, I savor the peace,
This rare and precious gift, I must release.

So let us cherish these moments we find,
When time is still and all is aligned.
For in them lies beauty, pure and true,
And memories we'll treasure, forever new.

An Introvert's Name List

I have seen that face
Seeming so familiar
Thinking of that, I can't find any trace
Even how hard I try
But that face
It is so familiar

Ah, now I know
He was that one person
With whom I used to talk over
It is just for college days
No, he was not interested in me
Neither was I

Just a simple cause of study
He needed something & I gave him
Math was his problem,
So was mine
And we connected there
For the sake of time

Now that four years have passed
And I am scrolling through the list
I came across a well-known chat
That chat comes to see
Showing me a few images of the past
That was still unclear to me.

Sorry friend, I apologize
It is all my fault your name is on an introvert's
list.
Who would never tell you, "Hi?"

Sunny afternoon
Shall a gentle, cold breeze flow
While watching the wind

Red Light, Green Light

It's late, late in the afternoon
I am three hours late
It'll be five when I reach home
The sun is already gone
This rain is not stopping at all
But stopping all my plans
My plans are floating in a boat
I can, see through the passing tree
The road is not the same; not it is only drenched
Now it is flowing with water
Beside the terrain

The view is all good until I sit in the bus
The bus is going to stop in the end, alas!
It stopped for me,
My window seat is empty now
I have to leave it as it is
My feet merged into the water
I raised the bag above my head
It's pouring heavily,
It can soak me in the rain
Hopping and jumping, I found a near-shade
Sheltering there I was waiting
Waiting for the lights to see again

The shade is lonely, like me,
Red lights, yellow lights, and green are all I see

Lights control everything
A car, a bus, and a walk
Moving and standing straight with the change of
check

It's a crossroad that connects four to five lanes
The one I'm going to has a little bend at the end

I am taking my time
Staying still under the shade
I'm coloring the lights in green

Drowsy

My body is leaning on a couch, and
So comfortable to feel, and
So tired
I am so sleepy, and
I can't open my eyes, and
The room is dark, and sounds aren't there and

I can't open my eyes, and
How hard I try and
They close automatically, and
I am drowning in sleep, and
Bits of thoughts are floating, and
Mostly are dangerous and
Mostly are from you and
I can't face them, and
Again, I jerked myself up and
That's how I've been sleeping for the last ten
days!

The sun is not peeking at us
Neither does the moon
It's another gloomy dawn
Filled with chills coming through the spine
Maybe a notation of an omen
It's just my guess
Maybe I am afraid
You're not here with me yet!

Burnt Bread

Sunny was the day, lighting the room
Through the glass window,
Making me happy again

I am telling you, I love the sun
Not only the heat but the rays that cover my
space
Making me happy again

Today is more special
Because it is new for me
I wake up late, without any hurry
Smelling baking bread and some scrambled eggs

Now you have become the man
And I am not on the front foot
You are taking the charge and
I will gladly accept your first half-burnt food.

Song of Dusk

As dusk descends, the world grows still,
Sunset hues dance upon the hill.
The day's hustle begins to fade,
In the embrace of twilight, memories are made.

Birds return to their cozy nests,
Stars emerge from their daytime rests.
A gentle breeze whispers its sigh,
As daylight bids, it's a soft goodbye.

Footsteps slow, hearts find their ease,
In the quiet hum of the evening breeze.
Fires flicker, casting shadows tall,
In its gentle thrall.

Dreams awaken, thoughts take flight,
Underneath the blanket of the night.
The day may end, but in its wake,
A world of possibilities awaits.

So let us cherish this twilight hour,
Embrace the calm, feel its power.
In the end, we find,
A moment of peace, serene and kind

People will grab you down
Don't let them touch your skin
Push them to the end of the bottom
Where the lights are in shades of neon green

Antara Chakraborty is a creative soul with more words to write and to speak. Born and raised in an urban area near Kolkata, she draws her inspirations from the beauty of nature, personal experiences, emotions and introspections. Summing them up she touches the hearts of her readers.

Have you written a book?
Publish it for free today!

Writer's Pocket is a publication house based in Vadodara, Gujarat. Established in 2016, we have a community of over 50,000 writers whose works we have published.

To publish your book with us for free, scan this QR code:

You can also reach out to us at:

Phone number: (+91) 8200 377 328
Email address: editor@writerspocket.com